HUNGRY FRED

HUNGRY FRED
by PAULA FOX
pictures by Rosemary Wells

Bradbury Press · Englewood Cliffs, New Jersey

For A.B.J.
and The Cupboard

Fred was hungry.
He ate the apples in the bowl on the table.

He ate the bowl.

Then he ate the table.

Fred was still hungry. He ate the rug in the dining room. Then he ate the dining room.

After that, he went out to the yard. He thought he would take a small nap.

But he was still hungry.

He ate the old birds' nests in the maple tree. Then he ate the maple
tree. He ate the three pine trees that stood near the fence. Then he ate
the fence. He sat down to rest.

But he was hungrier than ever. He went back and ate the rest of the
house. He ate the cellar.

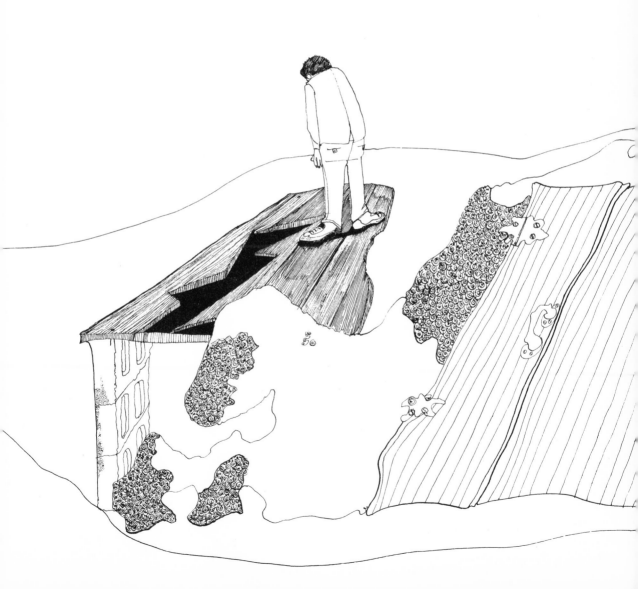

He also ate the furnace, the ping-pong table and an old ironing board.

Then he lay down next to the mulberry bush.

He looked all around. The house was gone. The trees were gone. The fence was gone. He ate the mulberry bush. Then that was gone.

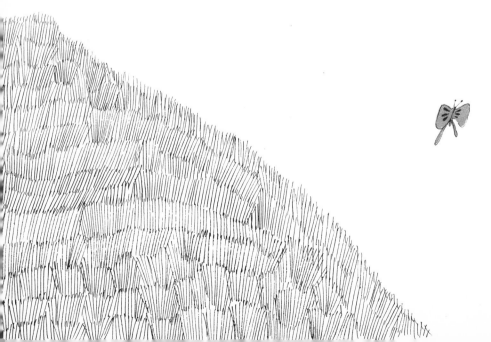

He walked across the meadow. On his way he stopped to eat the grass, the stones, the sticks, the flowers and an old wheel-barrow.

He came to the woods where he began to eat an oak tree.

A rabbit was looking at him. He stopped eating and walked toward it.

"Stay right there!" said the rabbit. "I've heard about you."

"I'm hungry," said Fred.

"We've all noticed that," said the rabbit.

"Who is *we?*" asked Fred.

"Everyone who lives in the woods," said the rabbit.

"I'm hungry right this minute," said Fred.

"I've got an idea," said the rabbit.

"What?" asked Fred.
"Let's take a walk," said the rabbit.
"Where?" asked Fred, looking at
a pine cone near the rabbit's foot.

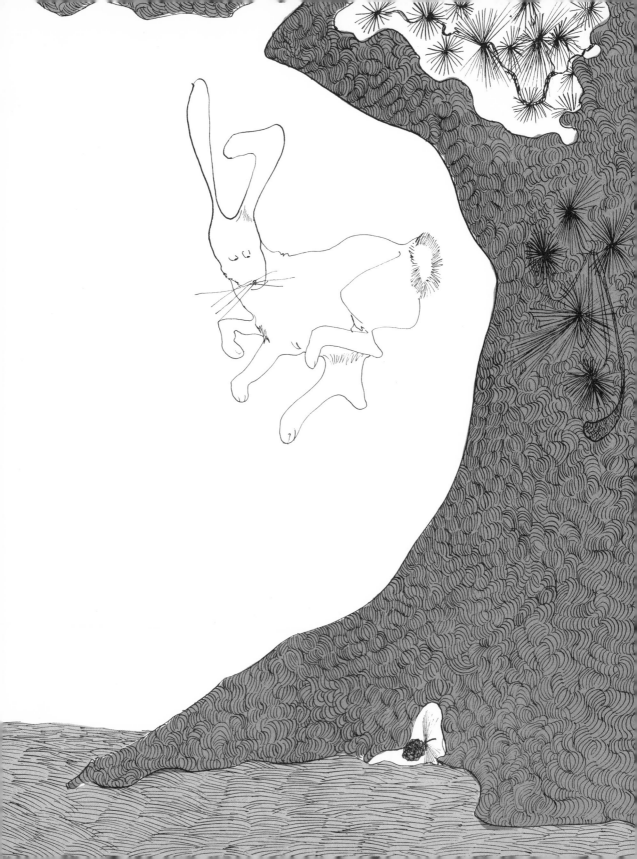

"That pine cone tastes awful," said the rabbit.
"How do you know?" asked Fred.
"I tried it," the rabbit answered.

"Okay," said Fred. "Where shall we walk?"
"How about going to your house?" suggested the rabbit.
"I ate it all up," said Fred.
"Perhaps you did," said the rabbit.

Fred and the rabbit walked back to where the house had been.

"Mercy!" said the rabbit. "What's going on?"
Fred's father was making a new clay fruit bowl.

Fred's big brother was building a ping-pong table.

Fred's big sister was knitting a rug.

Fred's mother was planting three pine trees, a maple tree and a mulberry bush.

"Say, you could live in one of those holes," said Fred.
"Say, I could, from time to time," answered the rabbit.

"Who's your friend?" asked Fred's father, pointing at the rabbit.

The rabbit leaned against Fred. Fred smiled. He felt full.